INCLUDING CHARACTERS FROM YOUR FAVORITE Disney·PIXAR FILMS

  Adventures in Learning

 Early Skills Collection

 Over 700 Educational Stickers!

★ Recognizing & Printing the Alphabet A to Z.

★ Recognizing, Matching & Writing Numbers 1 to 10.

Directions: Find the stickers that match the black and white images on each page. Then, complete the activities and use the reward stickers for added fun!

Bendon Publishing International, Inc.
Ashland, OH 44805
www.bendonpub.com

©2008 Disney Enterprises, Inc. and Pixar
All Rights Reserved

Matching and Printing Aa

First, find the stickers for the objects below (p.6). Then, follow the directions.

Name

Amazing Ants

Atta watches the ants. Capital **A** and small **a** are partner letters. Circle each ant that has partner letters. Then, trace and print the letters **A** and **a** on the lines.

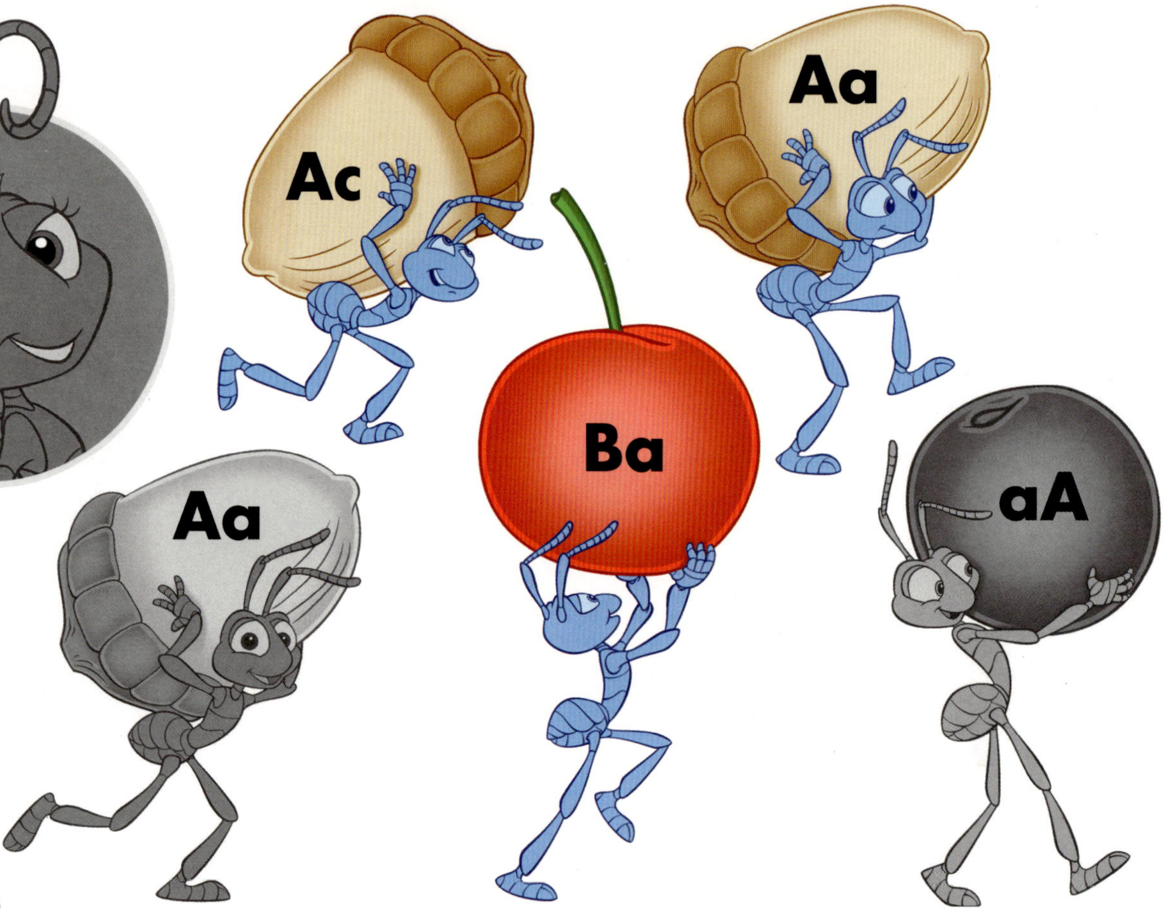

Answers on p.116

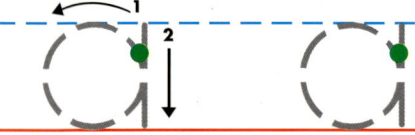

© Disney/Pixar

Recognizing and Printing Bb

First, find the sticker for the object below (p.6). Then, follow the directions.

Name

Belle's Books

Belle loves to read books. Color each book that has a capital **B** or small **b** on it. Then, trace and print the letters **B** and **b** on the lines.

Answers on p.116

© Disney/Pixar

Recognizing and Printing Cc

First, find the sticker for the object below (p.6). Then, follow the directions.

Name _____

Cinderella's Coach

Cinderella waves from her coach. Find and circle each capital **C** and small **c** in the picture. Then, trace and print the letters **C** and **c** on the lines.

Answers on p.116

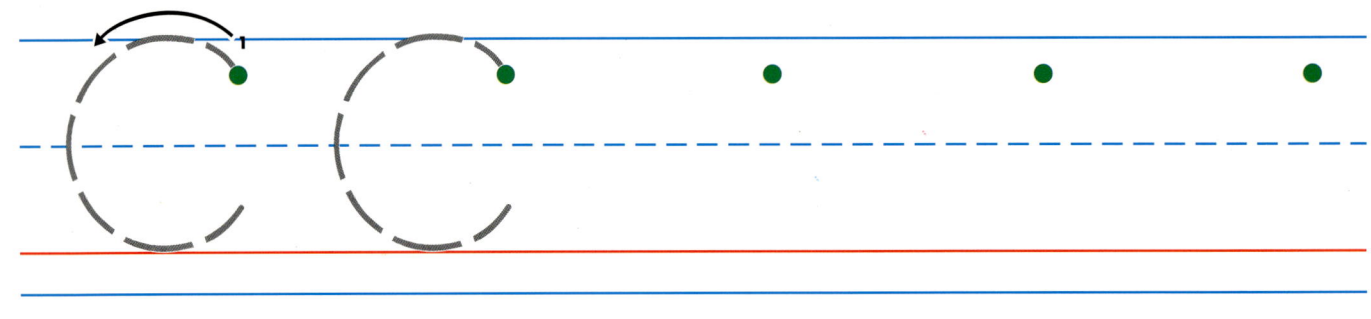

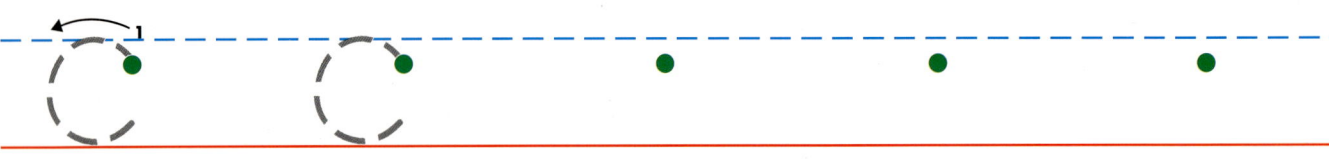

© Disney/Pixar

Stickers for pages 2, 3, and 4.

Stickers for pages 13, 14, 15 and 16.

Recognizing and Printing D d

First, find the stickers for the objects below (p.11). Then, follow the directions.

Name

Dandy Dinosaur

Help Rex figure out which of Andy's toys belong in the drawer. Draw a line from each picture that has a **D** or a **d** to the drawer. Then print the letters **D** and **d** on the lines.

Answers on p.116

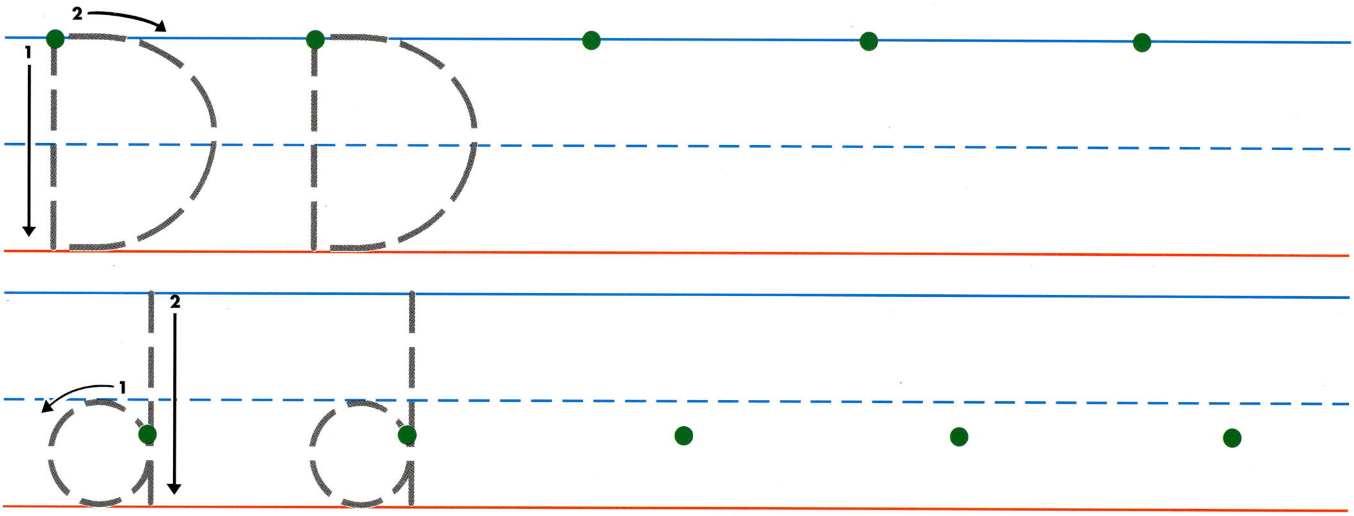

© Disney/Pixar

Recognizing and Printing E e

First, find the sticker for the object below (p.11). Then, follow the directions.

Name

Ears To You

Dumbo is a baby elephant with enormous ears. Circle all of the capital **E**'s and small **e**'s starting inside his ears. Then, trace and print the letters **E** and **e** on the lines.

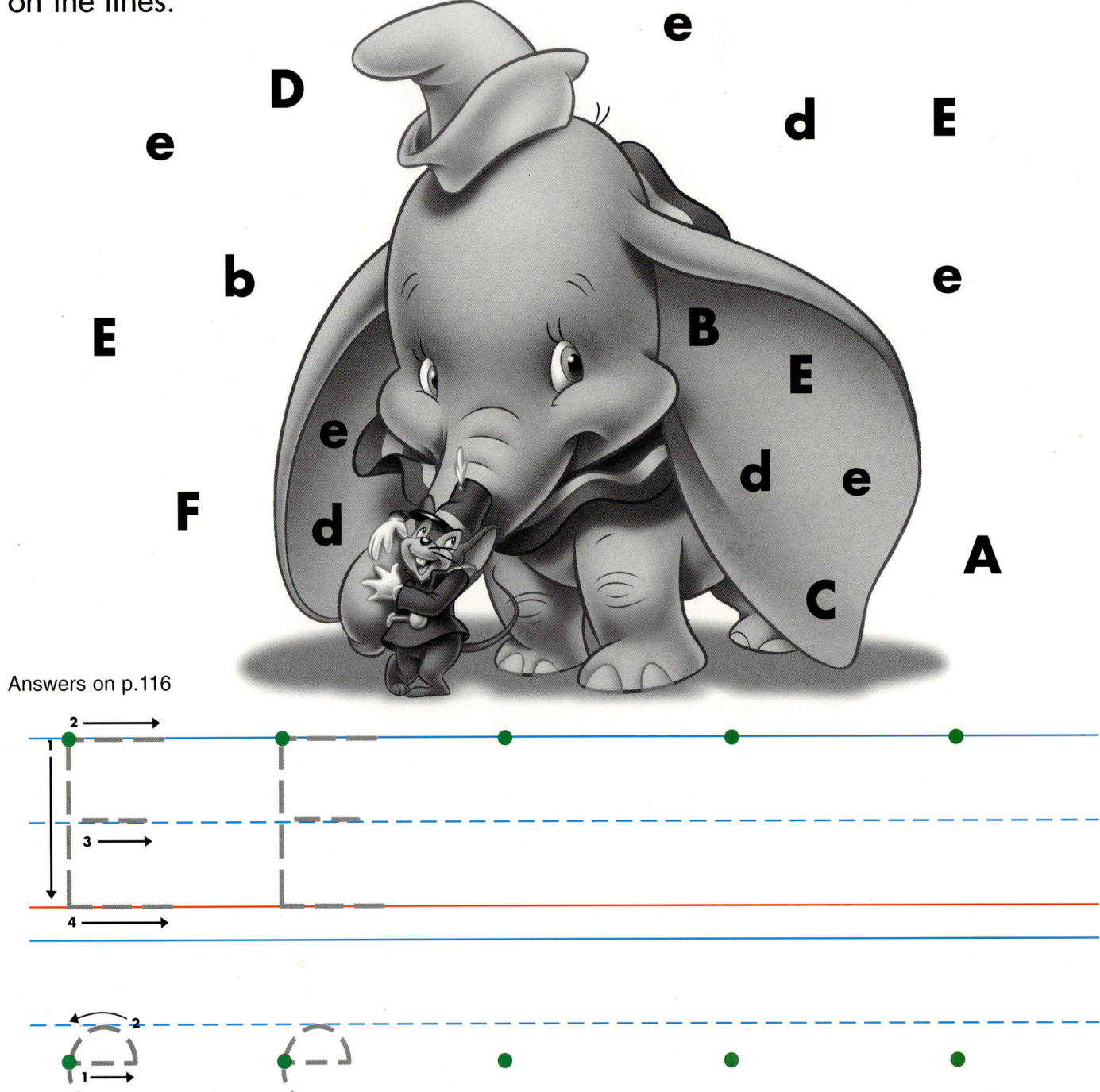

Answers on p.116

© Disney/Pixar

Recognizing and Printing F f

First, find the stickers for the objects below (p.11). Then, follow the directions.

Name

Friendly Fish

Ariel swims with some friendly fish. Color each fish that has an **F** or an **f** next to it. Then, trace and print the letters **F** and **f** on the lines.

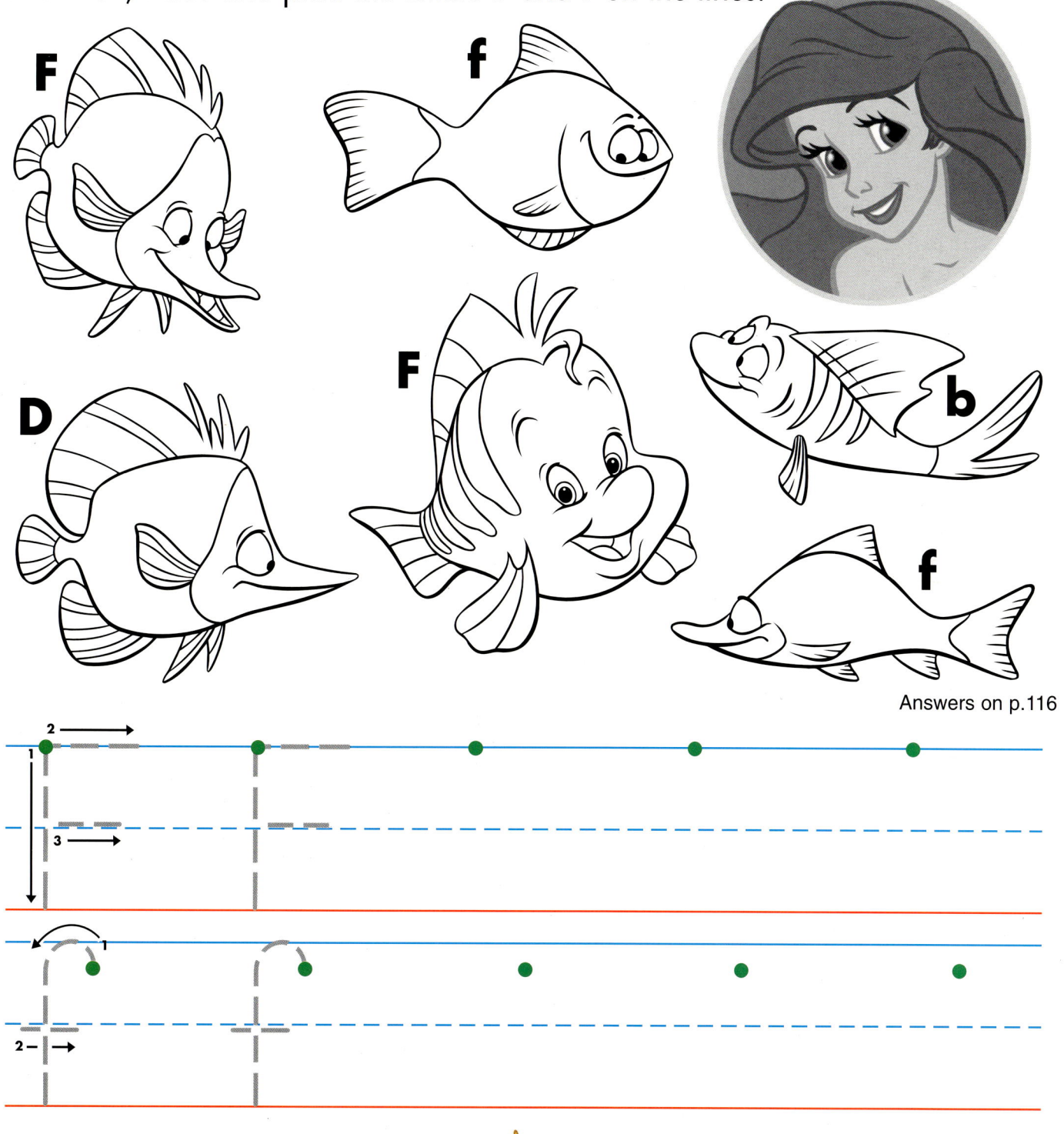

Answers on p.116

© Disney/Pixar

Matching and Printing Gg

First, find the sticker for the object below (p.11). Then, follow the directions.

Name

Goofy Games

Help Goofy play a matching game. Match each **G** on the inside of Goofy's drum to each **g** on the outside by drawing a line. Then, trace and print the letters **G** and **g** on the lines.

b

g

g

d

b

c

g

Answers on p.116

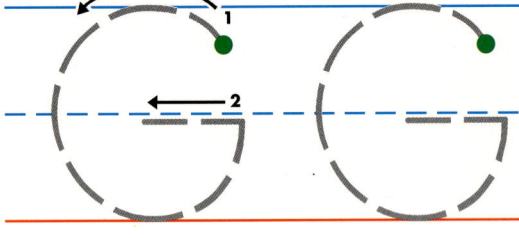

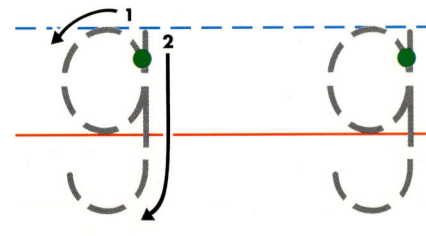

© Disney/Pixar

Recognizing and Printing Hh

First, find the sticker for the object below (p.30). Then, follow the directions.

Name

Hungry Horse

Help Phillipe find his food. Draw a line along the **Hh** path to get the horse to the hay. Then, trace and print the letters **H** and **h** on the lines.

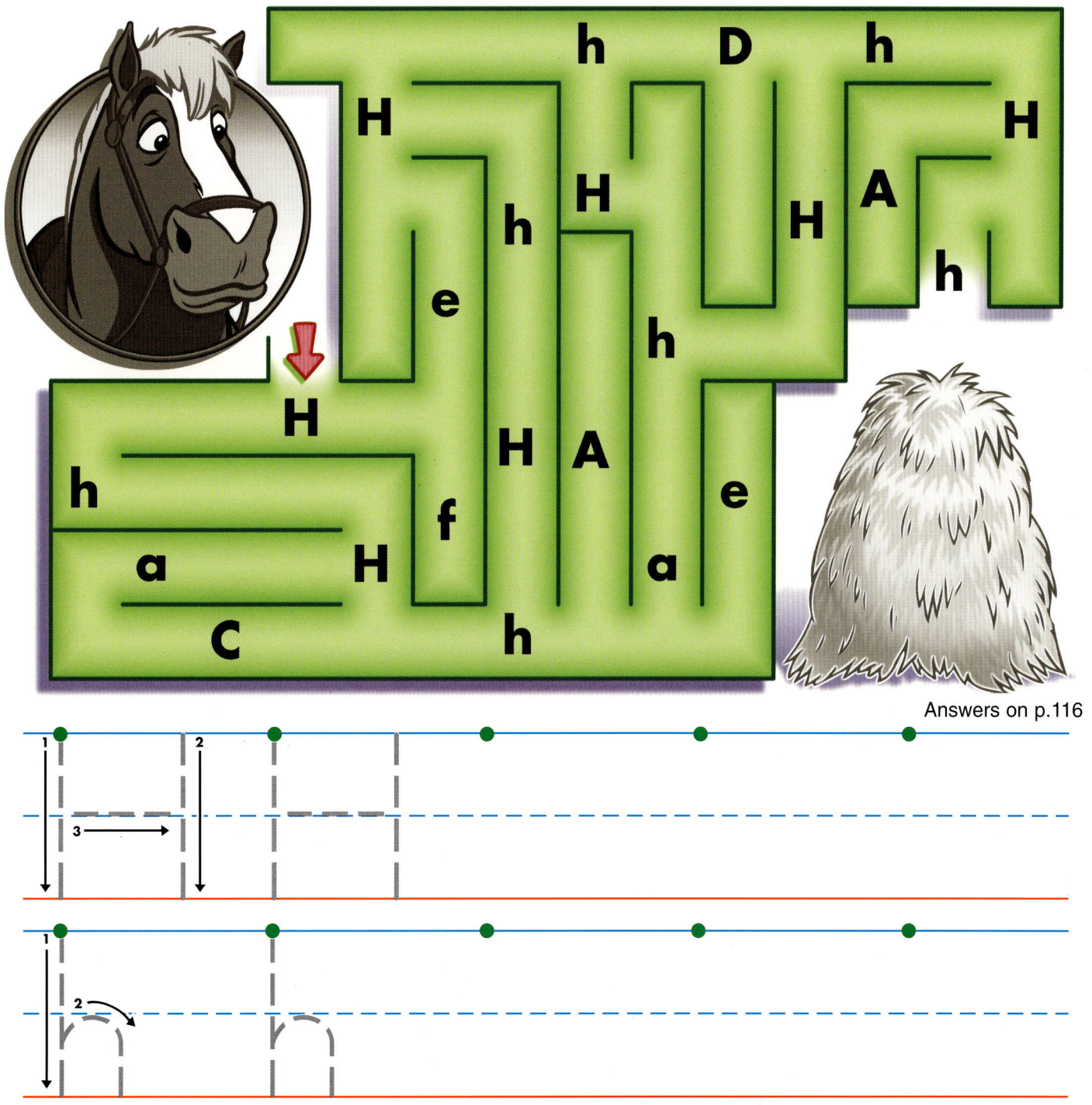

Answers on p.116

© Disney/Pixar

Matching and Printing I i

First, find the stickers for the objects below (p.30). Then, follow the directions.

Name

It's Icy

Bambi skates on the ice. Draw lines on the ice to match each capital **I** with a small **i**. Then, trace and print the letters **I** and **i** on the lines.

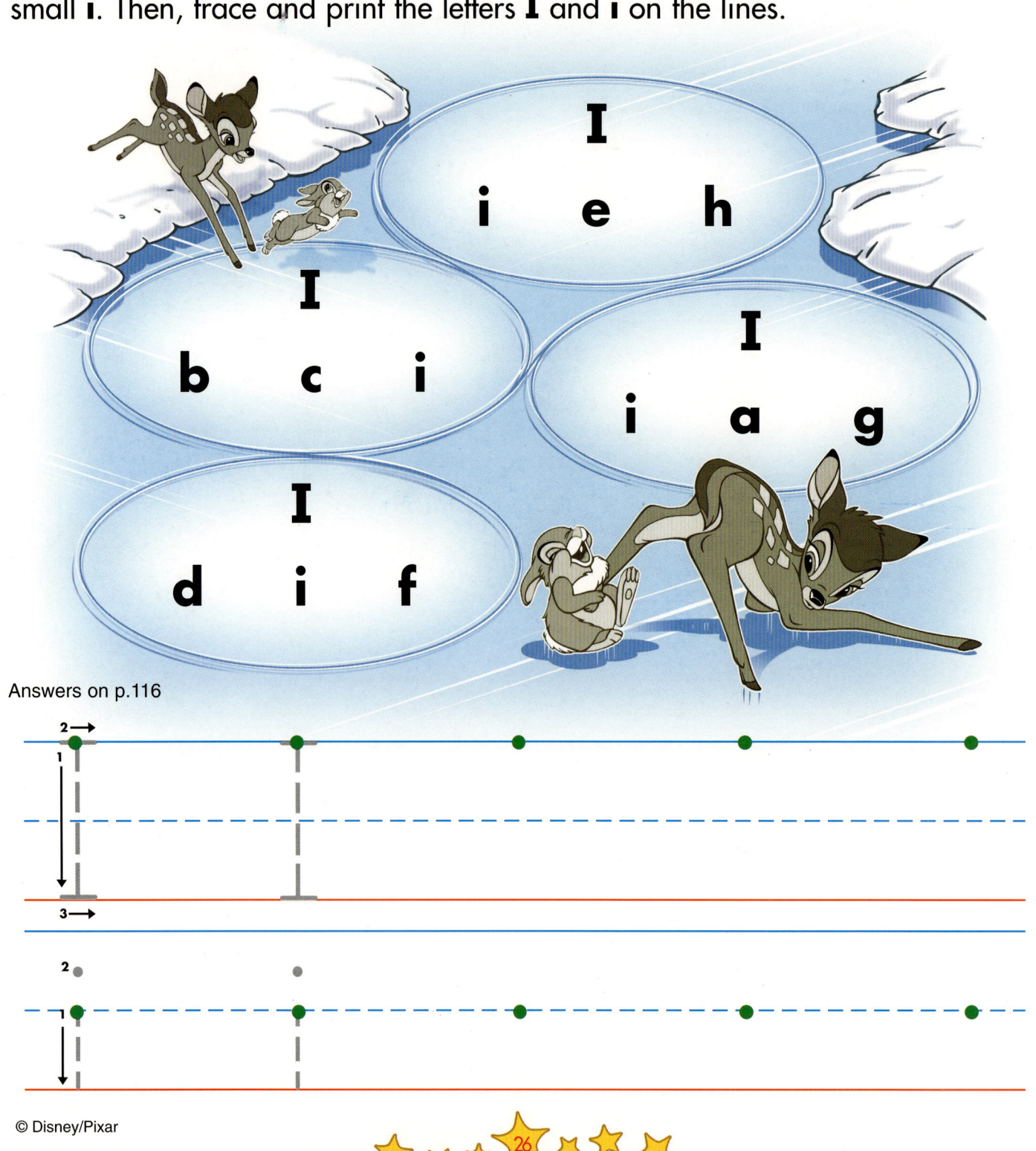

Answers on p.116

Recognizing and Printing Jj

First, find the sticker for the object below (p.30). Then, follow the directions.

Name

Just Jasmine

What is Princess Jasmine's favorite letter? Color each space that has a capital **J** or a small **j** on it to find out. Then, trace and print the letters **J** and **j** on the lines.

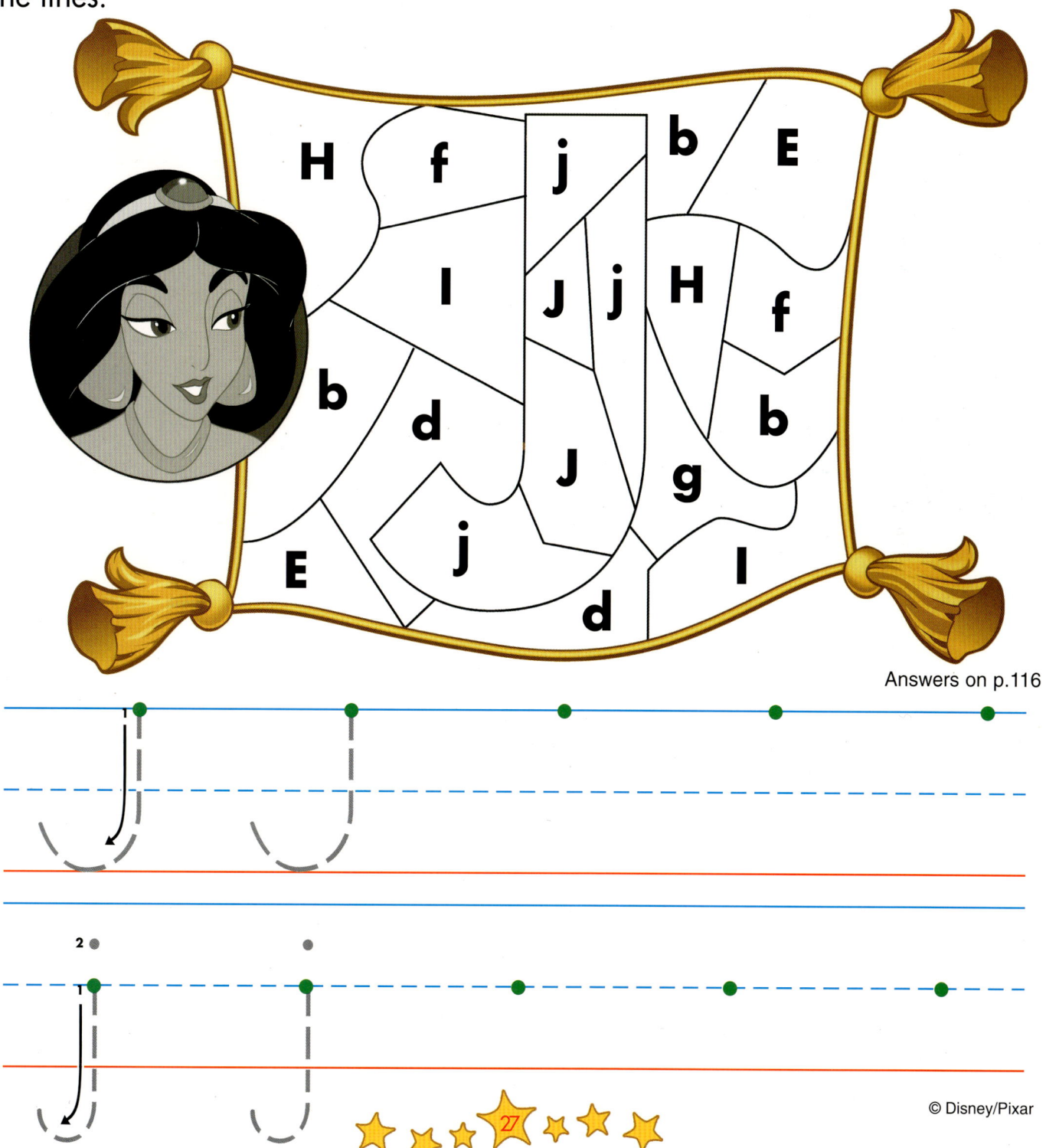

Answers on p.116

© Disney/Pixar

Recognizing and Printing Kk

First, find the sticker for the object below (p.30). Then, follow the directions.

Name

A Lion King

Mufasa is the Lion King. Help him show Simba the letter **K** by circling the lowercase **k**'s and capital **K**'s in the picture below. Then, trace and print the letters **K** and **k** on the lines.

Answers on p.116

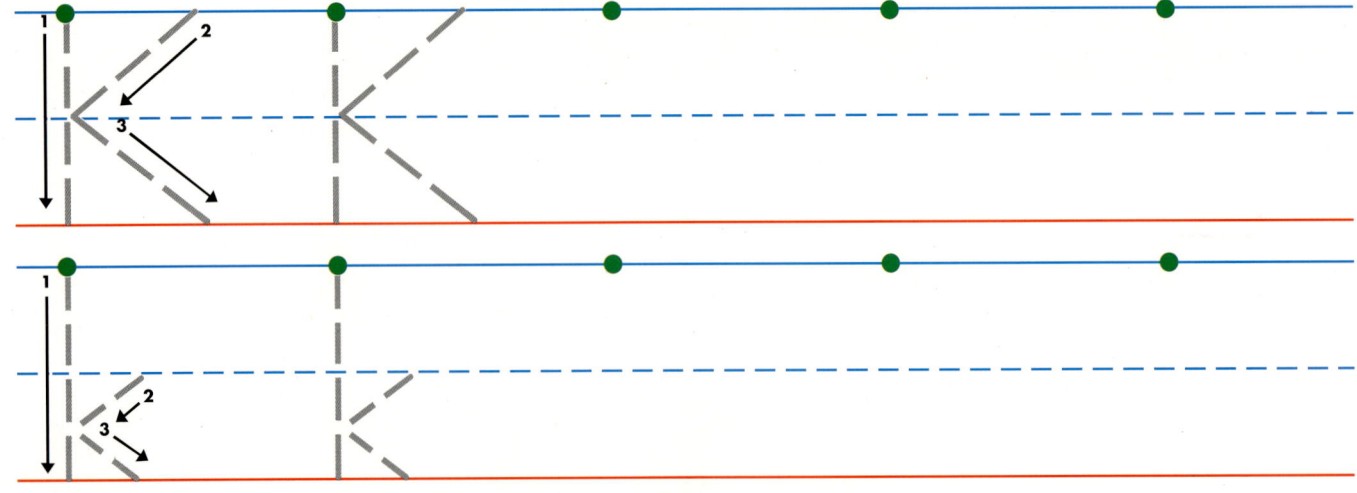

© Disney/Pixar

Stickers for pages 25, 26, 27 and 28.

Stickers for pages 37, 38, 39 and 40.

Recognizing and Printing Ll

First, find the sticker for the object below (p.35). Then, follow the directions.

Name

Lovely Leaves

Pocahontas loves to run through the leaves. Color each leaf that has an **L** or an **I** on it. Then, trace and print the letters **L** and **I** on the lines.

Answers on p.116

© Disney/Pixar

Recognizing and Printing Mm

First, find the stickers for the objects below (p.35). Then, follow the directions.

Name

Mini Monkey

Abu is a tiny, mini monkey. On each rug, circle the letter that is the same as the letter in the box. Then, trace and print the letters **M** and **m** on the lines.

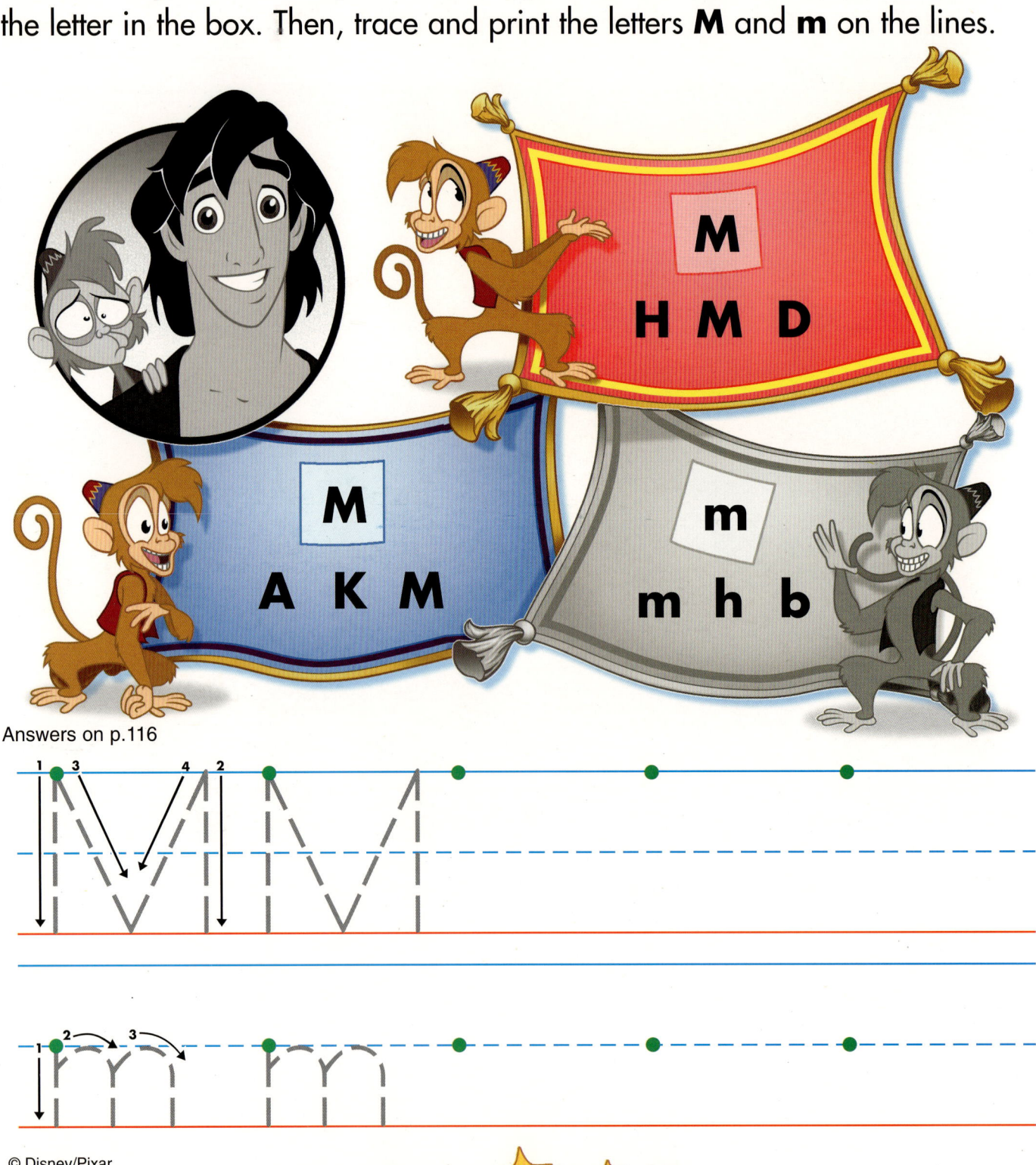

Answers on p.116

© Disney/Pixar

Matching and Printing Nn

First, find the stickers for the objects below (p.35). Then, follow the directions.

Name

Nibble on Nuts

Piglet may want to nibble on the nuts, but Pooh only wants to eat honey. Circle each nut that has capital **N** and small **n** on it. Then, trace and print the letters **N** and **n** on the lines.

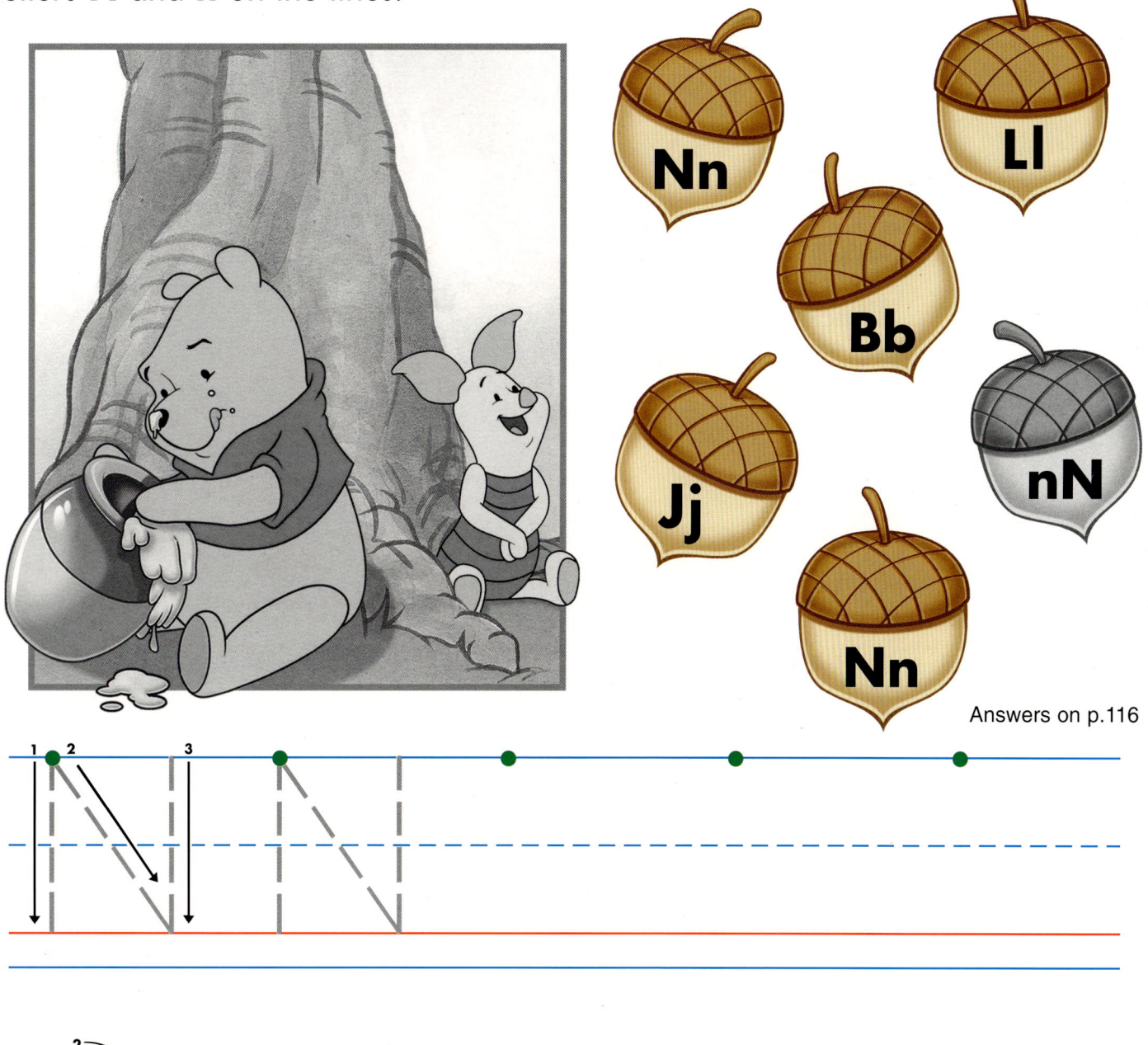

Answers on p.116

© Disney/Pixar

Recognizing and Printing Oo

First, find the sticker for the object below (p.35). Then, follow the directions.

Name

Orange Paint

Geppetto wants to open the orange paint. Draw a line along the **Oo** path to get Geppetto to the orange paint. Then, trace and print the letters **O** and **o** on the lines.

Answers on p.116

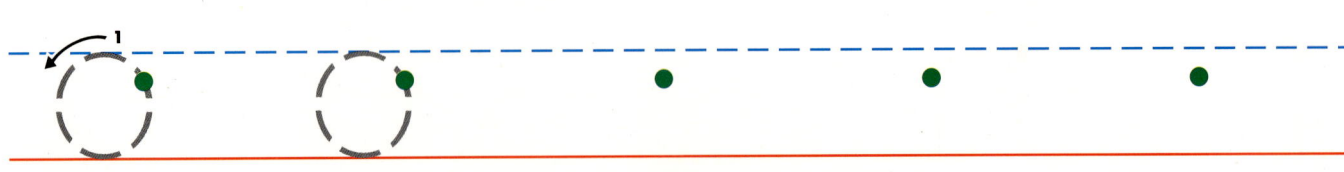

© Disney/Pixar

Recognizing and Printing P p

First, find the stickers for the objects below (p.54). Then, follow the directions.

Name

Playful Puppies

Pongo and Perdita's puppies like to play. Circle each puppy that has a **P** or a **p** under it. Then, trace and print the letters **P** and **p** on the lines.

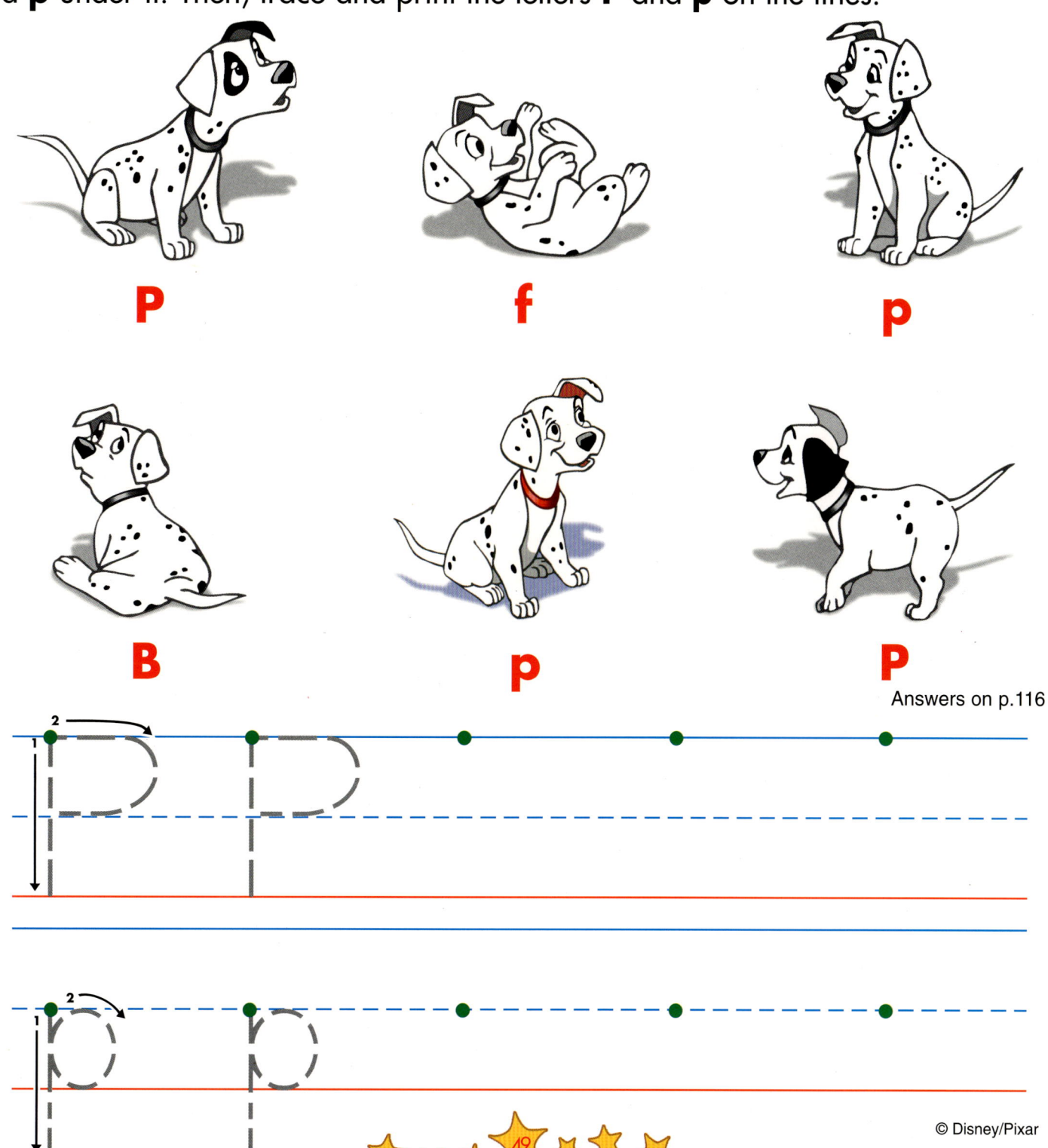

Answers on p.116

© Disney/Pixar

Matching and Printing Qq

First, find the sticker for the object below (p.54). Then, follow the directions.

Name

Question for the Queen

Atta asks the Queen a question. Color the question marks that have partner letters. Then, trace and print the letters **Q** and **q** on the lines.

What can we do, Mother?

Answers on p.116

© Disney/Pixar

Recognizing and Printing R r

First, find the sticker for the object below (p.54). Then, follow the directions.

Name

Really Rosy

What does Belle see in the jar? Color each space red that has a capital **R** or a small **r** on it. Then, trace and print the letters **R** and **r** on the lines.

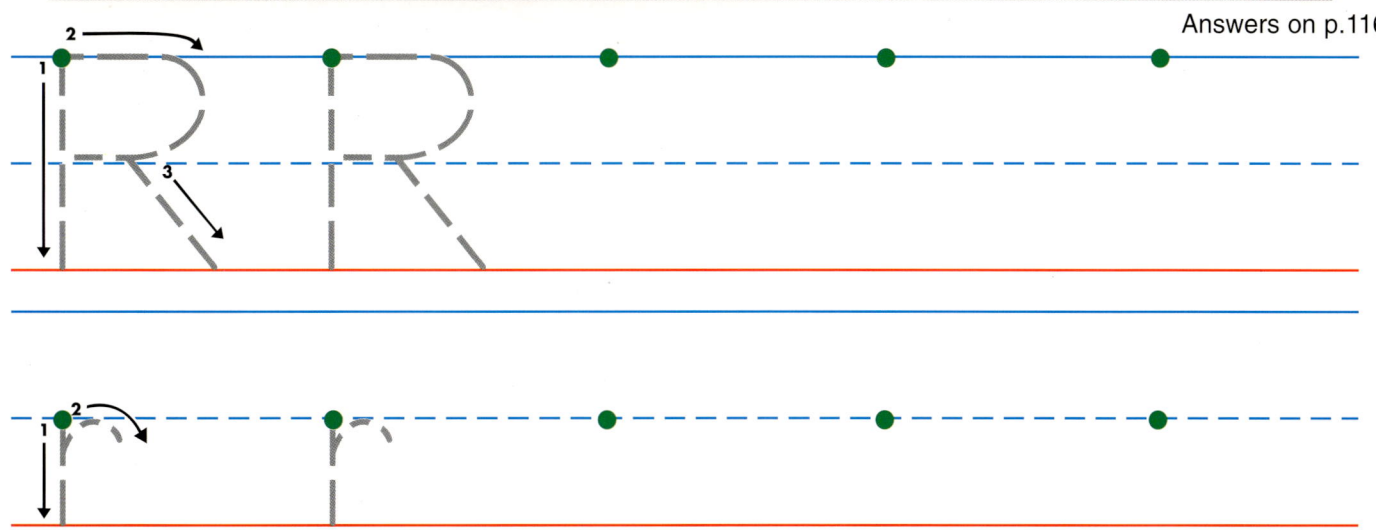

Answers on p.116

© Disney/Pixar

Recognizing and Printing S s

First, find the sticker for the object below (p.54). Then, follow the directions.

Sitting by the Sea

What does Ariel see by the sea? Circle each picture that has an **S** or an **s** on it. Then, trace and print the letters **S** and **s**.

Name

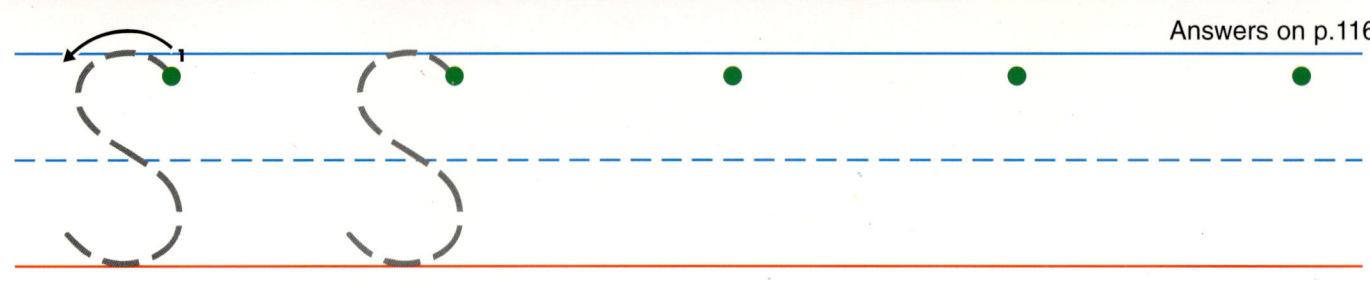

Answers on p.116

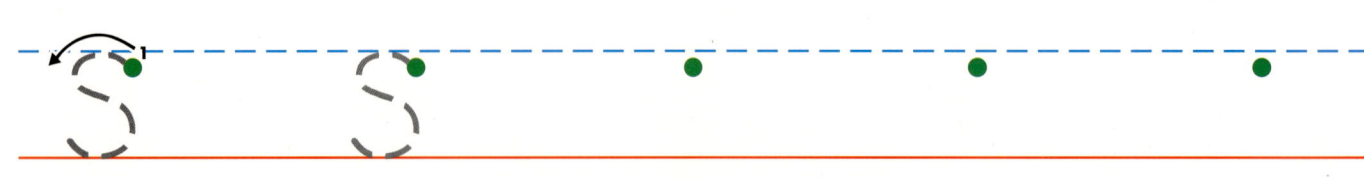

© Disney/Pixar

Stickers for pages 49, 50, 51 and 52.

Stickers for pages 61, 62, 63 and 64.

Matching and Printing Tt

First, find the sticker for the object below (p.59). Then, follow the directions.

Name

Time for Tea

It's Mrs. Potts and Chip's favorite time of day—tea time! Look at the letter **T** or **t** on each teapot. Color the teapot and the teacup that have partner letters. Then, trace and print the letters **T** and **t** on the lines.

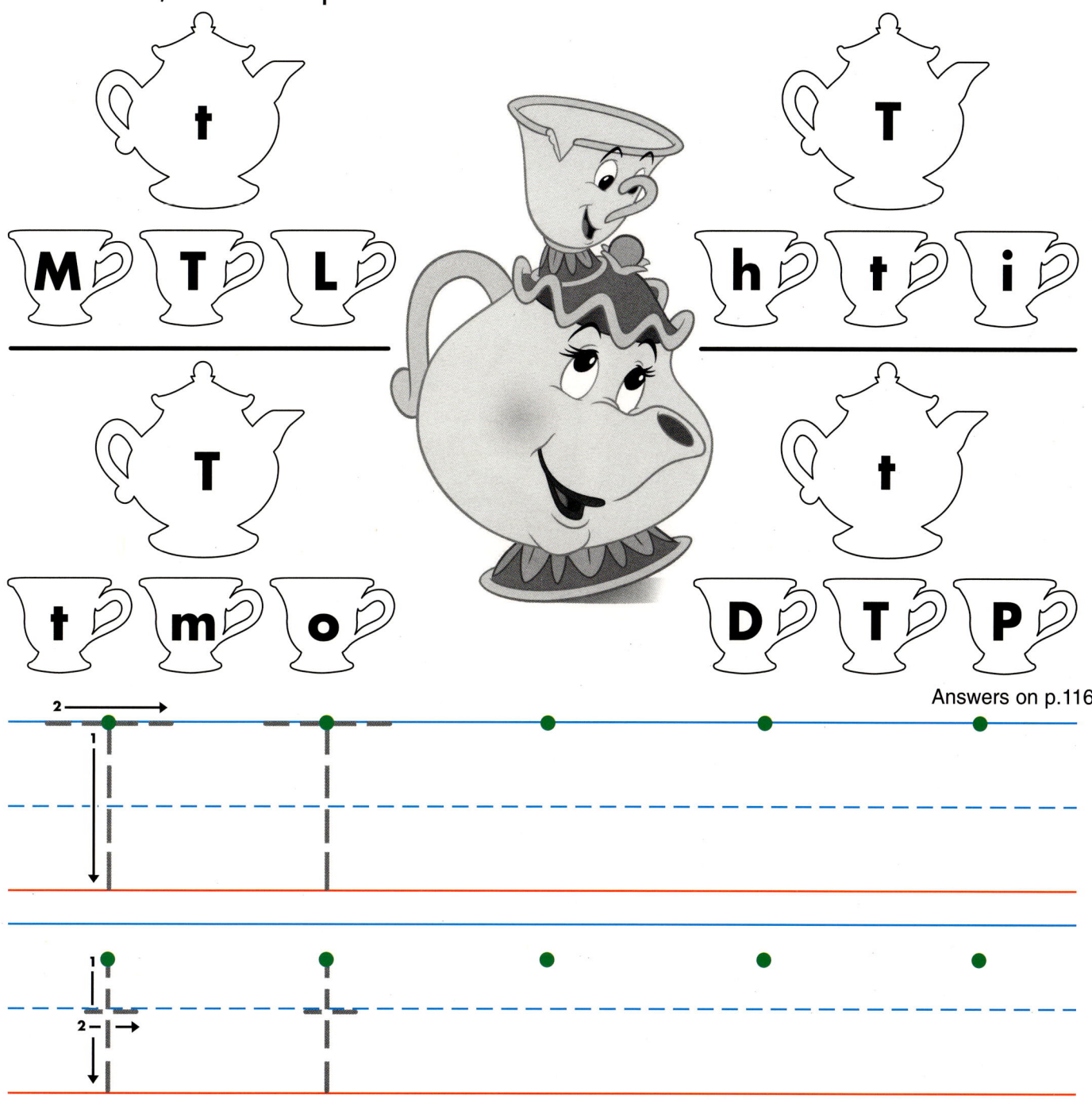

Answers on p.116

© Disney/Pixar

Recognizing and Printing U u

First, find the sticker for the object below (p.59). Then, follow the directions.

Up Goes the Umbrella

An umbrella keeps Pooh and Piglet dry. Color each part of the umbrella that has a capital **U** or a small **u** on it. Then, trace and print the letters **U** and **u** on the lines.

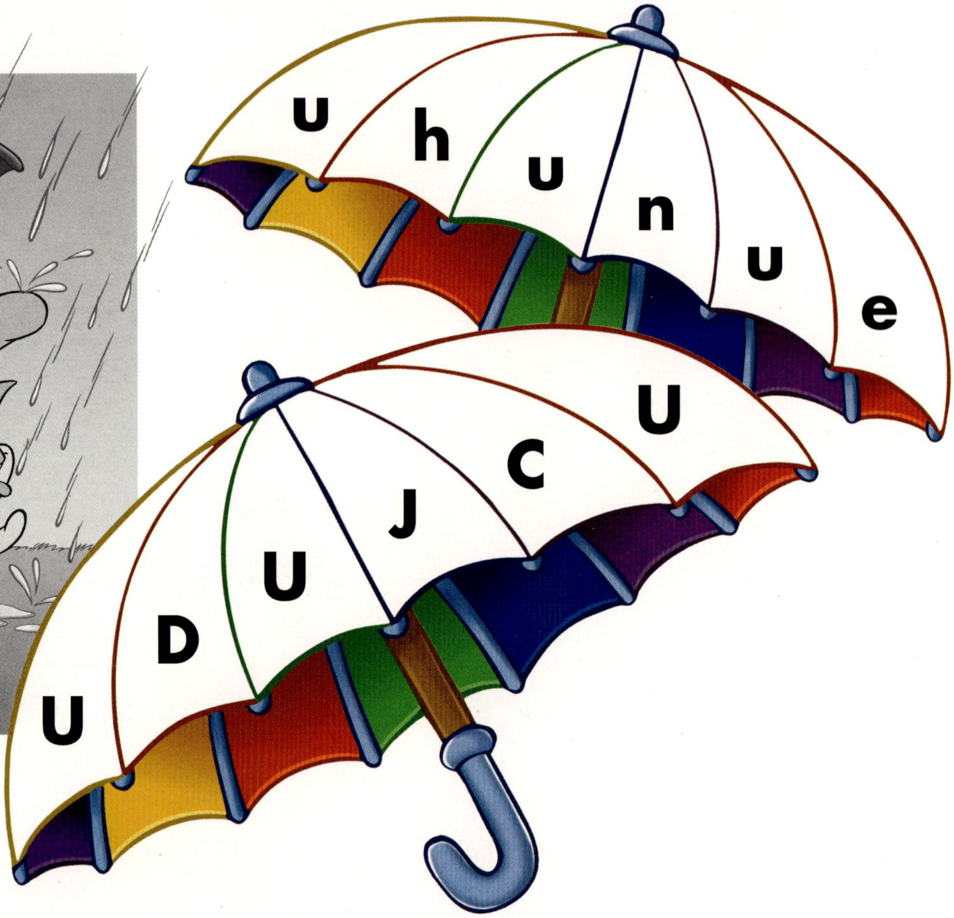

Answers on p.117

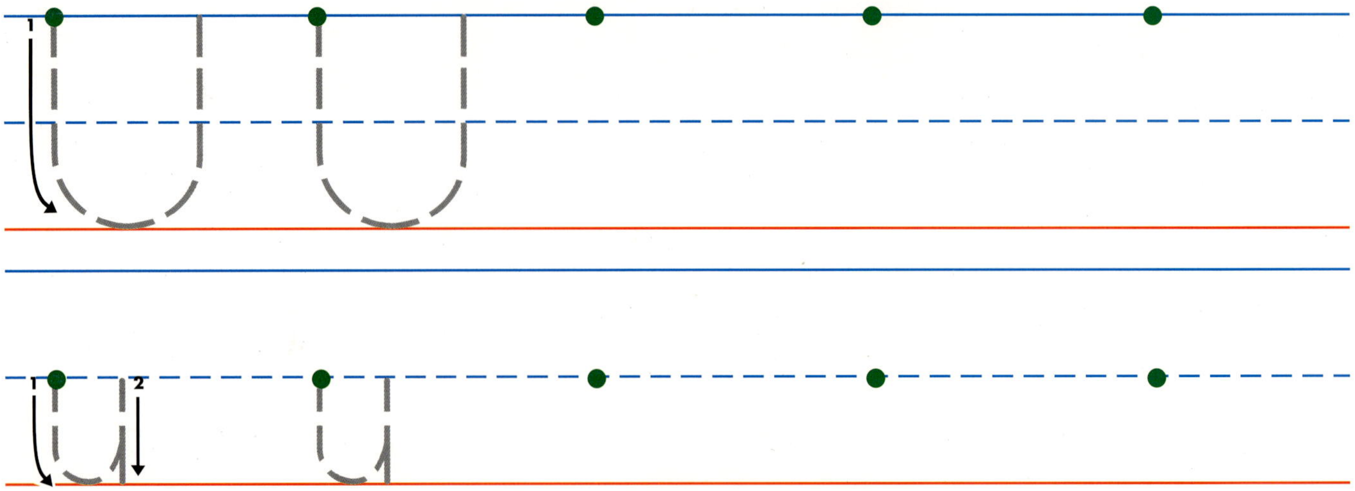

© Disney/Pixar

Recognizing and Printing Vv

First, find the sticker for the object below (p.59). Then, follow the directions.

Name

Very Much a Villain

Scar likes to create trouble. Circle each capital **V** and small **v**. Then, trace and print the letters **V** and **v** on the lines.

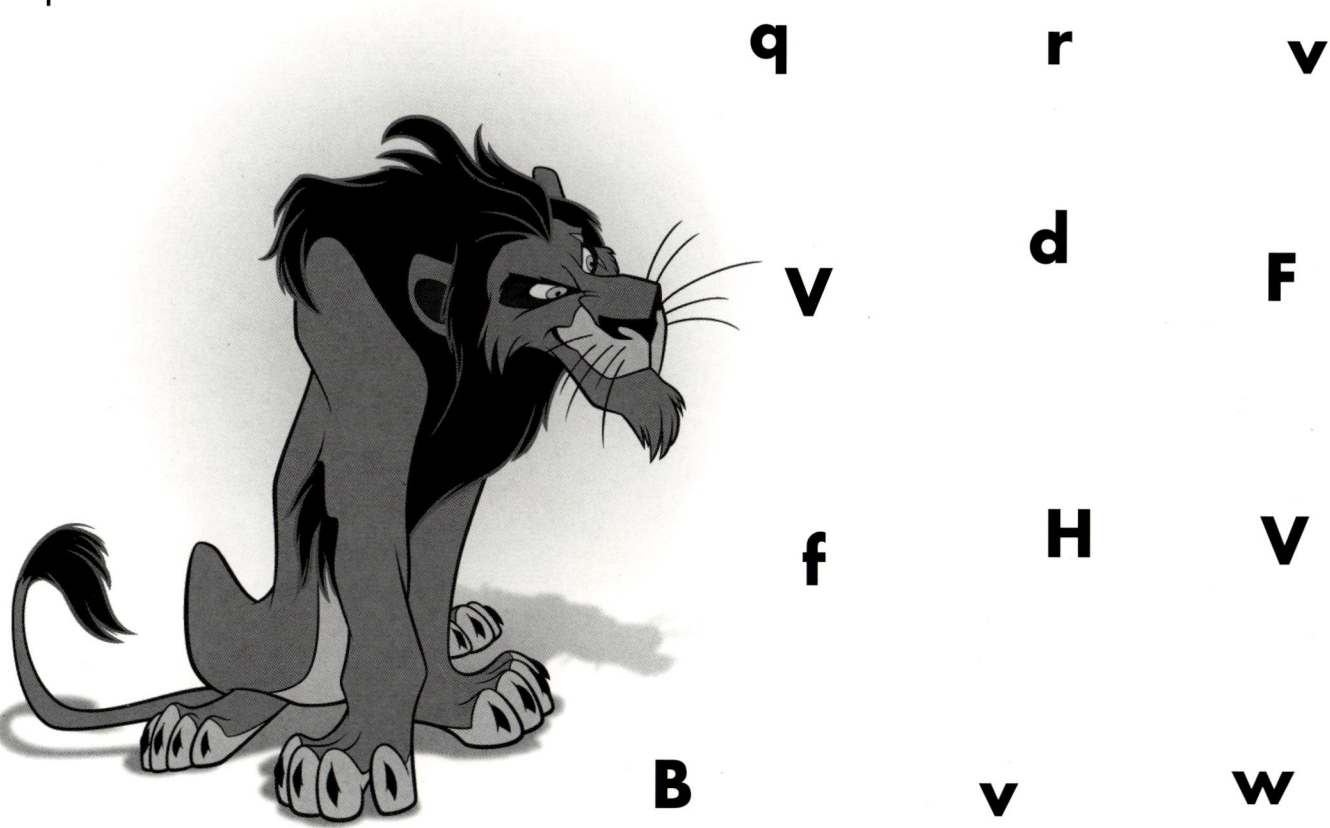

Answers on p.117

© Disney/Pixar

Recognizing and Printing Ww

First, find the stickers for the objects below (p.59). Then, follow the directions.

Woody's Window

What does Woody see outside the window? Circle each picture that has a **W** or a **w** next to it. Then, trace and print the letters **W** and **w** on the lines.

Answers on p.117

© Disney/Pixar

Recognizing and Printing Xx

First, find the stickers for the objects below (p.78). Then, follow the directions.

Name

Relax on a Box

The Seven Dwarfs are home from work. Now, they can relax. On each box, draw lines from the letter in the middle to the same two letters on that box. Then, trace and print the letters **X** and **x** on the lines.

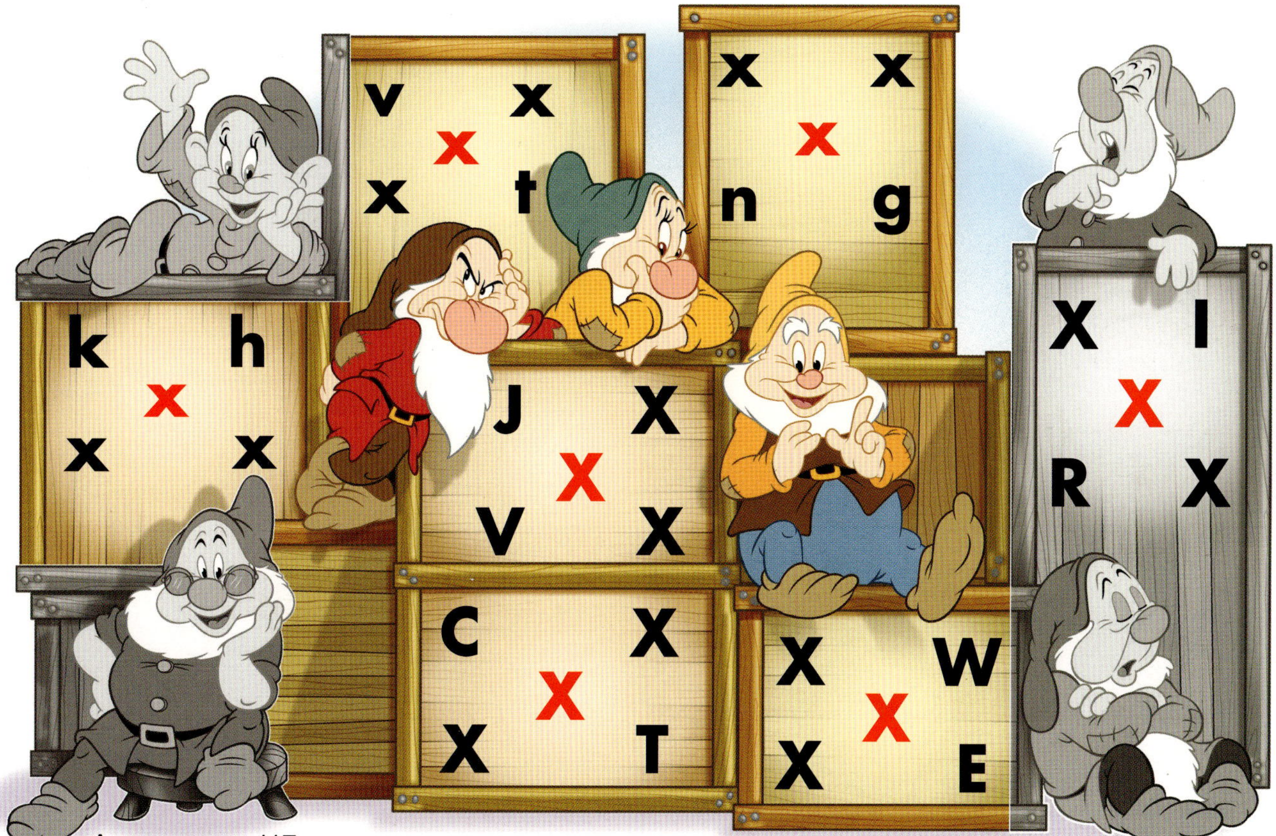

Answers on p.117

© Disney/Pixar

Recognizing and Printing Yy

First, find the stickers for the objects below (p.78). Then, follow the directions.

Name

Yes! He's in the Yard.

Help Andy find Buzz Lightyear. Draw a line along the **Yy** path through Andy's yard. Then, trace and print the letters **Y** and **y** on the lines.

Answers on p.117

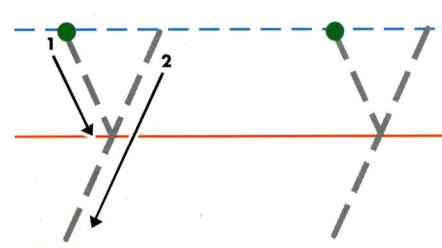

© Disney/Pixar

Recognizing and Printing Zz

First, find the sticker for the object below (p.78). Then, follow the directions.

Name _____

Zazu Can Zigzag

Zazu can zigzag from tree to tree. Cross out each letter that is not a **Z** or a **z**. Then, trace and print the letters **Z** and **z** on the lines.

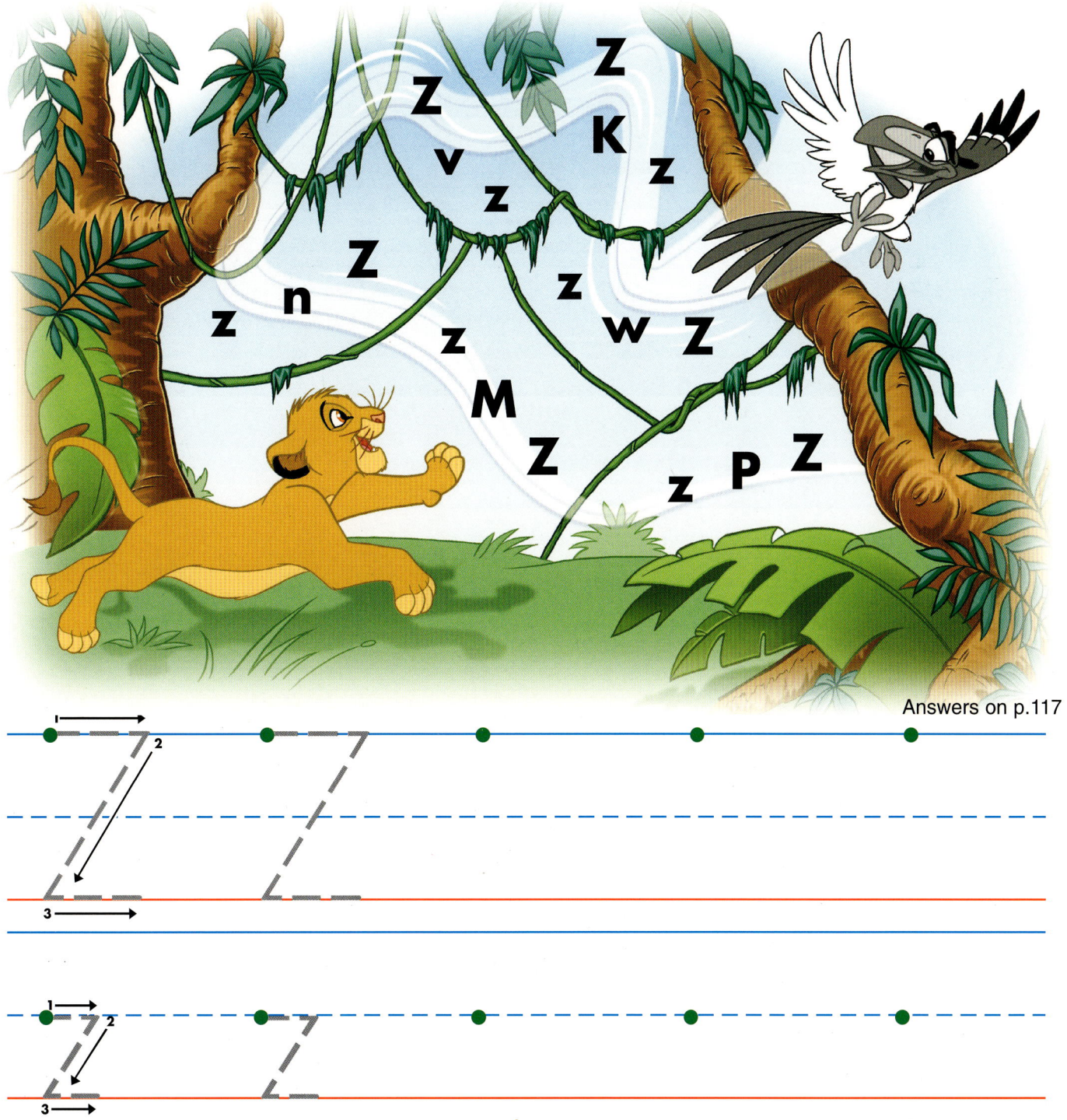

Answers on p.117

© Disney/Pixar

Recognizing and Writing 1

First, find the stickers for the objects below (p.78). Then, follow the directions.

Buzz Is Number 1

Circle the pictures that show 1.
Then, trace and write the number **1**.

  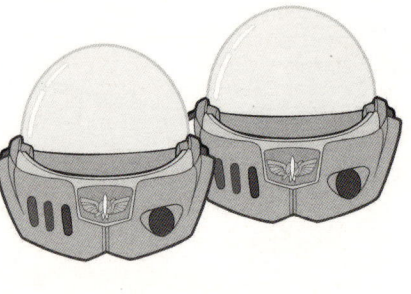

Answers on p.117

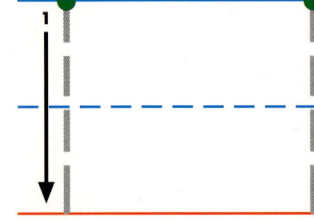

© Disney/Pixar

Stickers for pages 73, 74, 75 and 76.

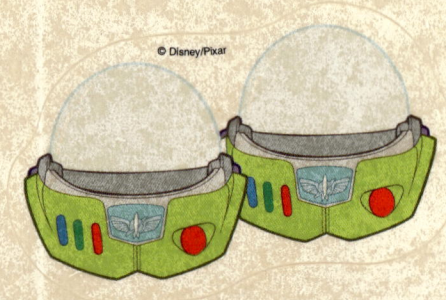

Stickers for pages 85, 86, 87 and 88.

Recognizing and Writing 2

First, find the sticker for the object below (p.83). Then, follow the directions.

2 at a Time

Name

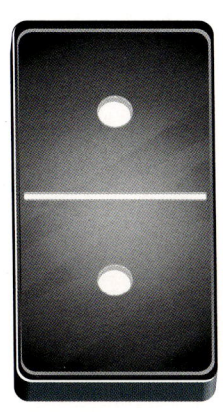

Can you find 2 Dalmatians?
Circle each group of 2. Then, trace and write the number **2**.

Answers on p.117

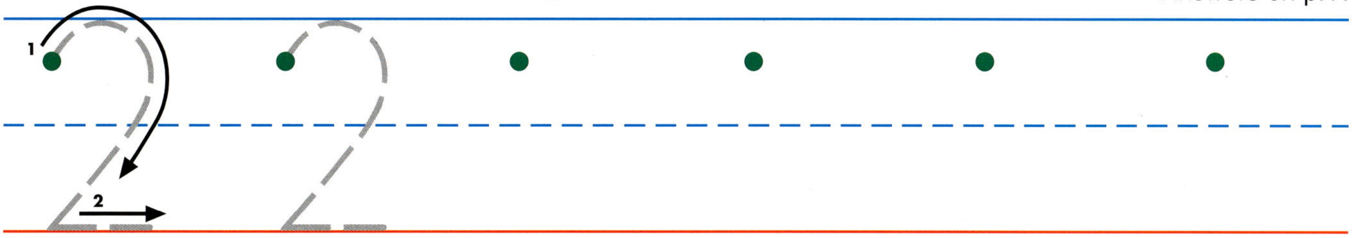

© Disney/Pixar

Recognizing and Writing 3

First, find the stickers for the objects below (p.83). Then, follow the directions.

Do You See 3?

Name _____

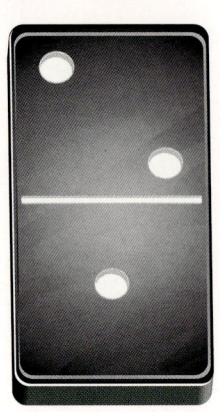

Help Mater count the tires. Circle each group of 3. Then, trace and write the number **3**.

Answers on p.117

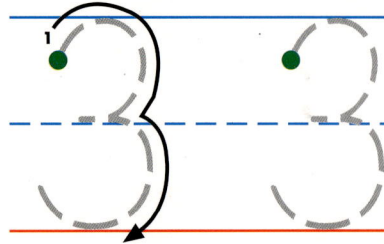

© Disney/Pixar

Recognizing and Writing 4

First, find the sticker for the object below (p.83). Then, follow the directions.

4 in a Row

Name

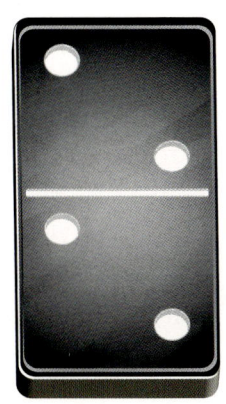

Help Timon and Pumbaa count the footprints below. Count and circle **4** footprints in each row. Then, trace and write the number **4**.

Answers on p.117

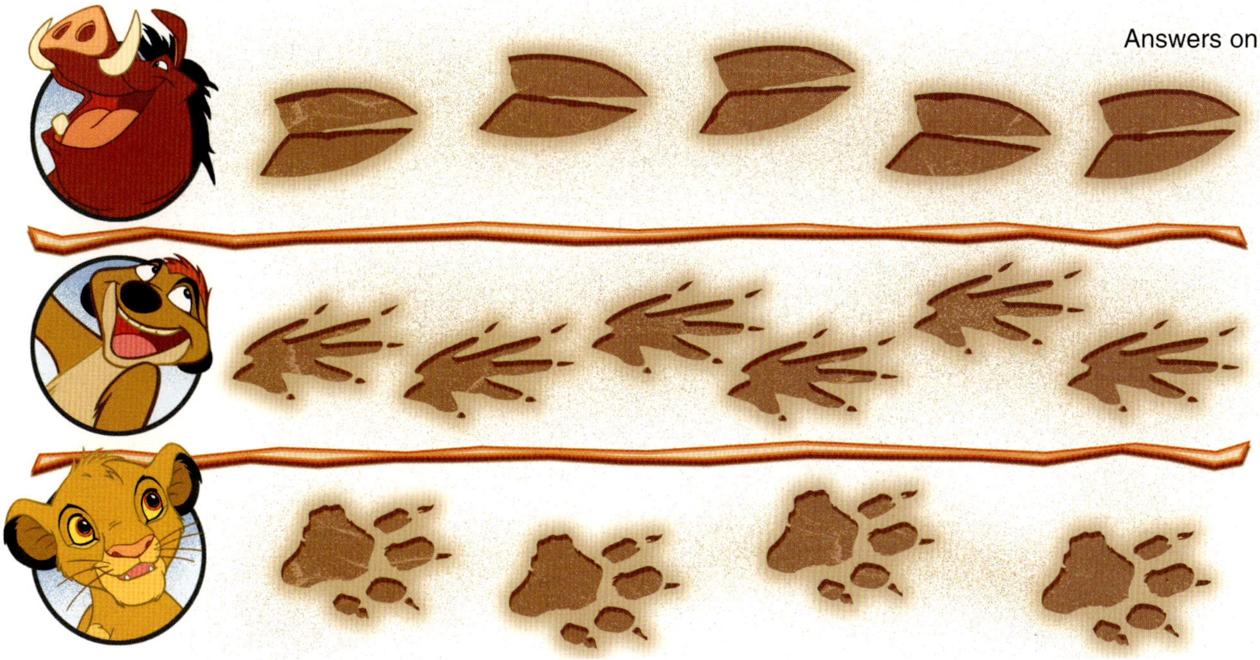

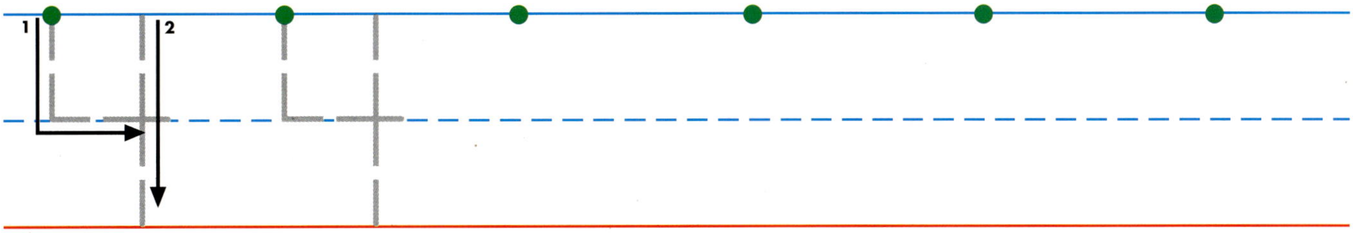

© Disney/Pixar

Recognizing and Writing 5

First, find the stickers for the objects below (p.83). Then, follow the directions.

5 Fun Foods

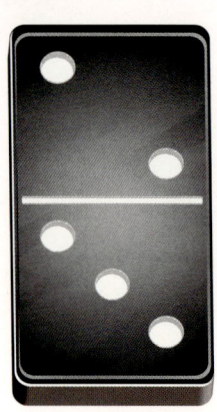

Name

Heimlich loves the circus! What can you see and do at a circus? First, circle 5 foods. Then, trace and write the number **5**.

Answers on p.117

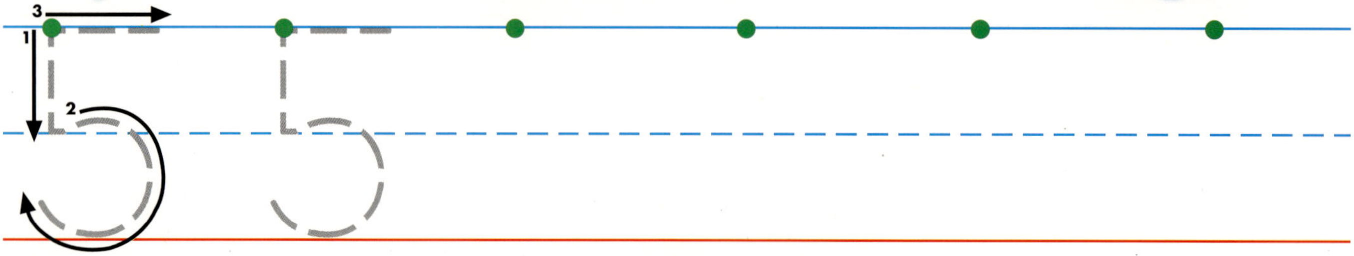

© Disney/Pixar

Ordinals First Through Fifth

First, find the sticker for the object below (p.102). Then, follow the directions.

Name _____

Today's Talent Show

Pooh and his friends are having a talent show. They will all win a ribbon. Follow the directions below.

Color the **third** ribbon 🟨.   Color the **fourth** ribbon 🟩.

Color the **fifth** ribbon 🟧.   Color the **second** ribbon 🟥.

Color the **first** ribbon ⬛.

Answers on p.117

© Disney/Pixar

Recognizing and Writing 6

First, find the sticker for the object below (p.102). Then, follow the directions.

Pick 6

 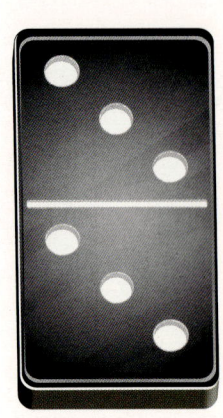 

Name

Pooh will show Piglet how to make a kite. There are 6 circles on Pooh's kite. Color each kite that has 6 shapes on it. Then, trace and write the number **6**.

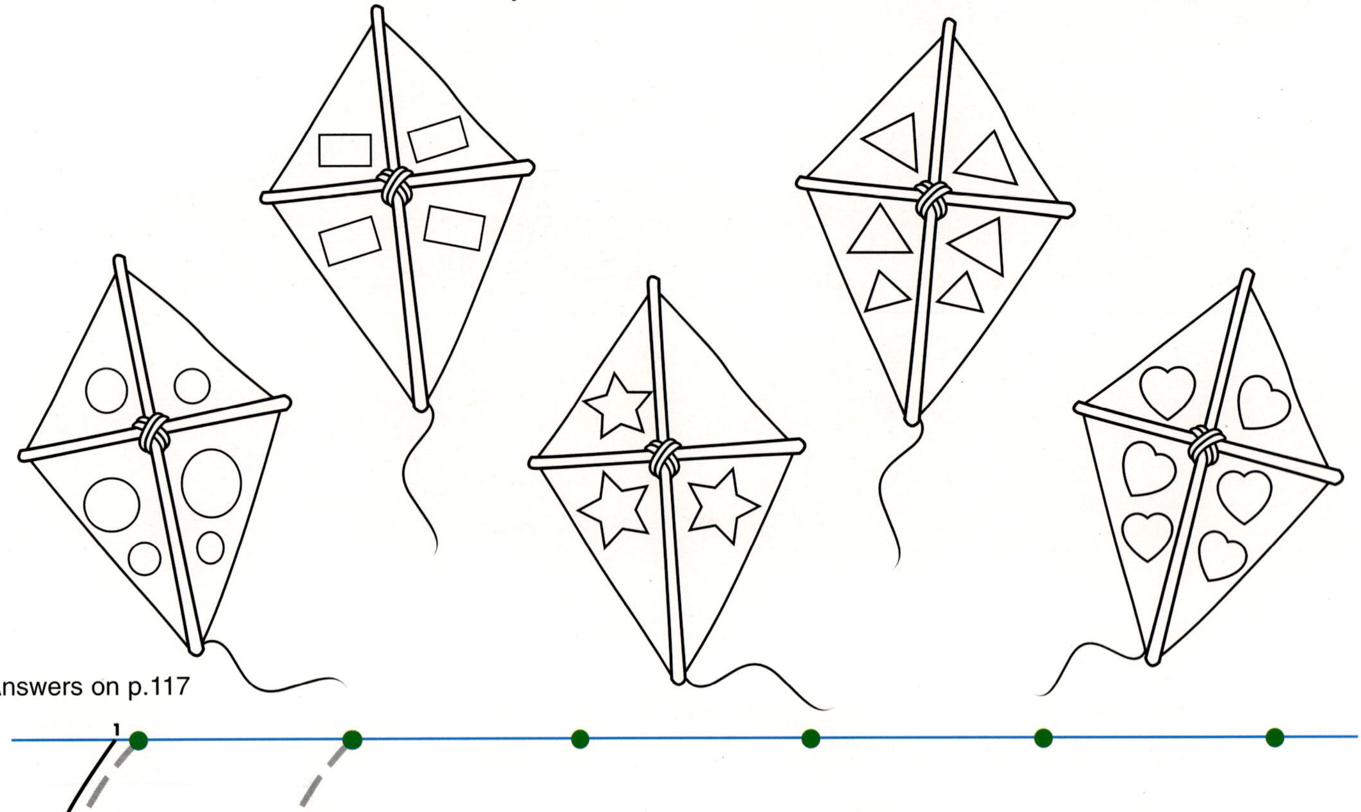

Answers on p.117

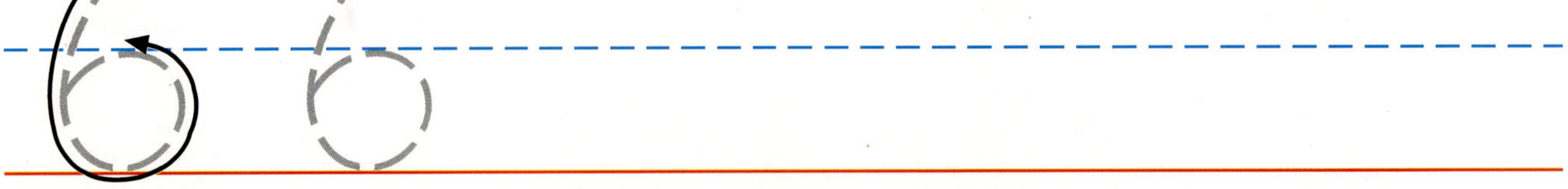

© Disney/Pixar

Recognizing and Writing 7

First, find the sticker for the object below (p.102). Then, follow the directions.

7 Silly Hats

Name

Can you count how many Dwarfs there are? Of course, there are 7. Count and color 7 hats. Then, trace and write the number **7**.

Answers on p.117

© Disney/Pixar

Recognizing and Writing 8

First, find the sticker for the object below (p.102). Then, follow the directions.

Wait for 8

 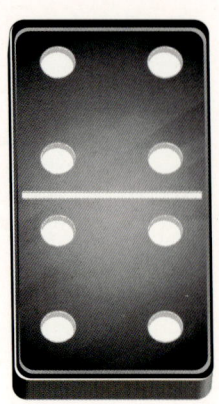 

Name

Lightning loves to see the checkered flag at the finish line. Count how many flags you see below. Then, trace and write the number **8**.

© Disney/Pixar

Stickers for pages 97, 98, 99 and 100.

Beautiful work!

Well done!

Stickers for pages 109, 110, 111 and 112.

Recognizing and Writing 9

First, find the sticker for the object below (p.107). Then, follow the directions.

9 Is Nice

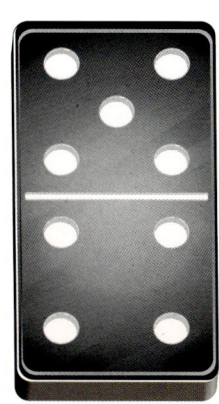

Name

Count the things in each group. Draw a line from each group that has 9 things to the number **9**. Then, trace and write the number **9**.

Answers on p.117

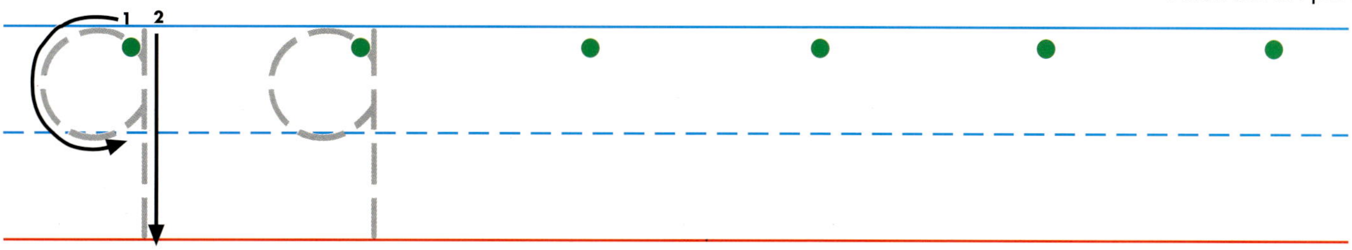

© Disney/Pixar

Recognizing and Writing 10

First, find the stickers for the objects below (p.107). Then, follow the directions.

10 Is Tricky

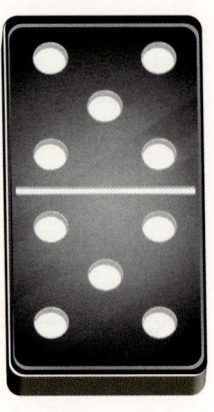

Name

Try a trick like Manny does. Draw 10 legs on the bug. Then, make it turn a different color. **Hint:** Your crayons will help you do this trick! Then, trace and write the number **10**.

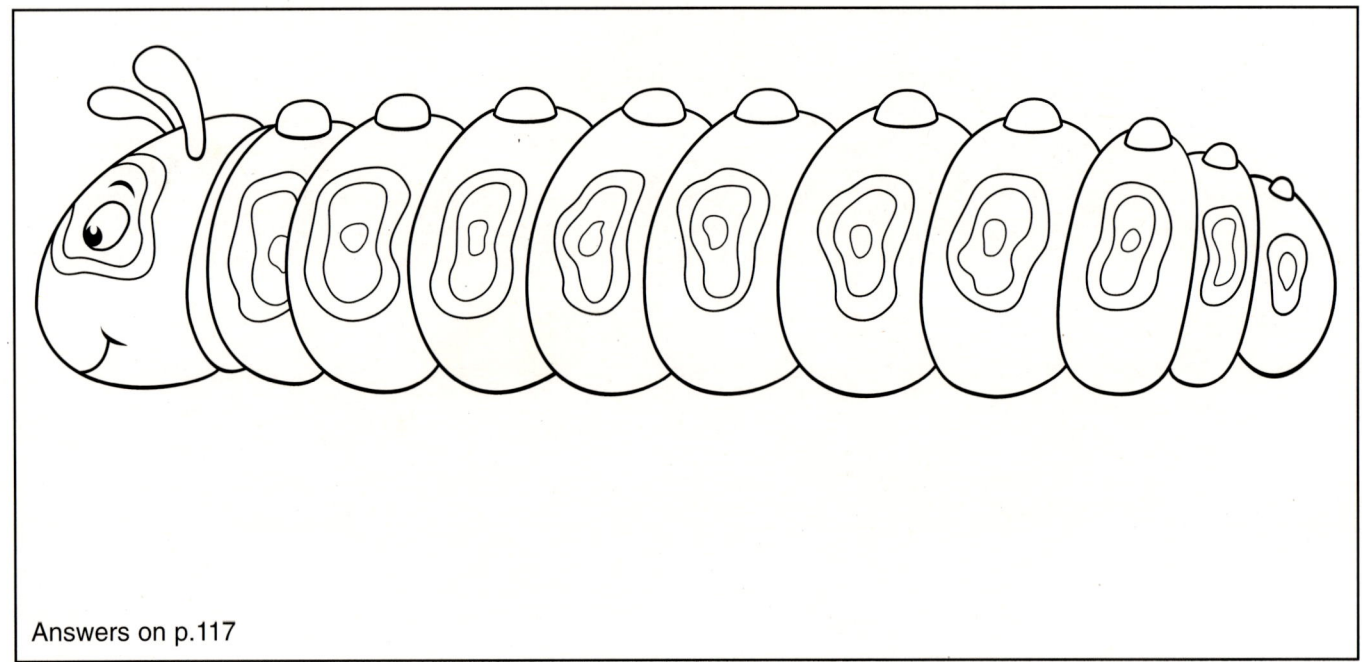

Answers on p.117

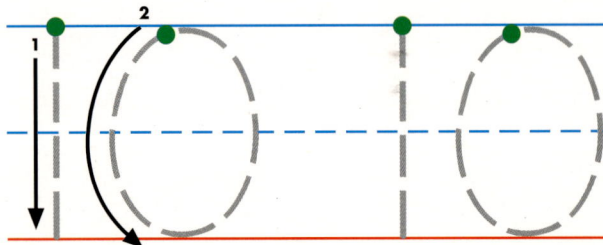

© Disney/Pixar

Ordinals Sixth Through Tenth

First, find the sticker for the object below (p.107). Then, follow the directions.

Name _____

Let's Visit Bambi

Ten animals are waiting to visit Bambi. Beginning with Flower, point to the **sixth**, **seventh**, **eighth**, **ninth**, and **tenth** animal in line. Then, follow the directions below. Start with Flower. Circle the **sixth** animal. Draw a box around the **eighth** animal. Draw an **X** on the **tenth** animal.

Answers on p.117

© Disney/Pixar

Reviewing Ordinals First

First, find the stickers for the objects below (p.107). Then, follow the directions.

Name

Follow the Path

Help Aladdin get to Princess Jasmine along the path of lamps. Follow the directions below.

Color the **first** lamp 🟩. Color the **seventh** lamp 🟦.
Color the **fourth** lamp 🟥. Color the **tenth** lamp 🟨.

Answers on p.117

© Disney/Pixar

Answer Key

Page 2

Page 3

Page 4

Page 13

Page 14

Page 15

Page 16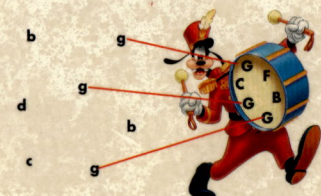

Page 25

Page 26

Page 27

Page 28

Page 37

Page 38

Page 39

Page 40

Page 49

Page 50

Page 51

Page 52

Page 61

© Disney/Pixar

Answer Key

Page 62

Page 63

Page 64

Page 73

Page 74

Page 75

Page 76

Page 85

Page 86
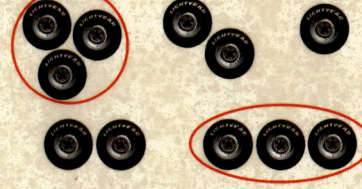

Page 87
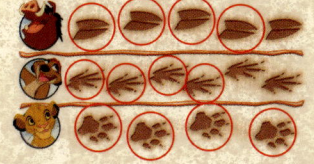

Page 88
Any 5 pictures may be circled.

Page 97

Page 98
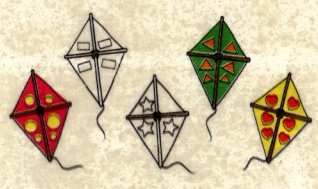

Page 99
Any 7 hats may be colored.

Page 109

Page 110

Page 111

Page 112

© Disney/Pixar